When We Were Alone

David Alexander Robertson
Julie Flett

HIGHWATER PRESS

Today I helped my kókom in her flower garden. She always wears colourful clothes. It's like she dresses in rainbows. When she bent down to prune some of the flowers, I couldn't even see her because she blended in with them. She was like a chameleon.

"Nókom, why do you wear so many colours?" I asked.

Nókom said, "Well, Nósisim…"

When I was your age, at home in my community, my friends and I wore many different colours. But at the school I went to, far away from home, they gave us different clothes to wear. All the children were dressed the same, and our clothes weren't colourful at all. We all mixed together like storm clouds.

"Why did you have to dress like that?" I asked.
"They didn't like that we wore such beautiful colours," Nókom said. "They wanted us to look like everybody else."

But sometimes in the fall, when we were alone, and the leaves had turned to their warm autumn hues, we would roll around on the ground. We would pile the leaves over the clothes they had given us, and we would be colourful again.

And this made us happy.

"Now," Nókom said, "I always wear the most beautiful colours."

After I helped with the flowers, we went over to the back gate. There were vines covering the gate, and they reached all the way to the ground. When my kókom turned to fix the latch, I saw that her braid hung almost as low as the vines. It was like she had a tail.

"Nókom, why do you wear your hair so long?" I asked.

Nókom said, "Well, Nósisim…"

When I was your age, at home in my community, my friends and I grew our hair long, just like our people have always done. It made us feel strong and proud. But at the school I went to, far away from home, they cut off all our hair. Our strands of hair mixed together on the ground like blades of dead grass.

"Why did you have to wear your hair like that?"
I asked.

"They didn't like that we were proud," Nókom said.
"They wanted us to be like everybody else."

But sometimes in the spring, when we were alone, and the grass had grown so long and thick in the field, we would pick the blades from the ground. We would braid them into the short hair they had given us, and we would have long hair again.

And this made us happy.

"Now," Nókom said, "I always wear my hair very long."

After my kókom had fixed the latch, I followed her to the birdhouse. There was a bird flying through the air like a jingle-dress dancer. She fed the bird and whispered, "Na pinaysis, miciso, ta misi kitiyin, ta maskisiyin,"* and her words sounded just like a poem.

"Nókom, why do you speak in Cree?" I asked.

Nókom said, "Well, Nósisim…"

*"Here little bird, eat, so you will get big and strong."

Na pinaysis, miciso,

ta misi kitiyin,

ta maskisiyin

When I was your age, at home in my community, my friends and I always spoke our language. But at the school I went to, far away from home, they wouldn't let us speak our words. All the children used *their* strange words, and we didn't understand them at all. Our voices blended together like a flock of crows.

"Why did you have to talk in their language?" I asked.

"They didn't like that we spoke our language," Nókom said. "They wanted us to talk like everybody else."

But sometimes in the summer, when we were alone, and our teachers weren't anywhere around the place we were, we would whisper to each other in Cree. We would say all the words we weren't allowed to say so that we wouldn't forget them.

And this made us happy.

"Now," Nókom said, "I always speak my language."

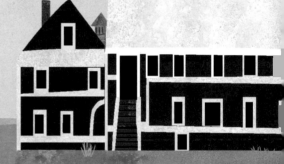

After our gardening work was done, I sat with my kókom in the backyard. Her brother came over and sat with us. He comes over all the time. We drank tea and ate bannock. The tea was hot and sweet, and the bannock was moist and warm and melted in my mouth. My kókom and my uncle talked and laughed like children.

"Nókom, why do you and Nókomis always spend time together?" I asked.

Nókom said, "Well, Nósisim…"

When we were your age, at home in our community, being with family was the most important thing. We played with each other, did chores together, and shared everything. But at the school I went to, far away from home, they wouldn't let us be together.

My brother and I were separated like day and night.

"Why were you and Nókomis separated?" I asked.

"They didn't like when we were with family," Nókom said, "because when we were together we thought too much of home."

But sometimes in the winter, when we were alone, and we were sure that nobody could see us, we would find each other. We would take off our mitts, and in the crisp, cold air we would hold hands so we could be with each other.

And this made us happy.

"Now," Nókom said as she reached over and held my uncle's hand, and mine, "I am always with my family."

HighWater Press gratefully acknowledges the financial support of the Province of Manitoba through the Department of Sport, Culture & Heritage and the Manitoba Book Publishing Tax Credit, and the Government of Canada through the Canada Book Fund (CBF) for our publishing activities.

The publisher also acknowledges the support of the Canada Council for the Arts, which last year invested $153 million to bring the arts to Canadians throughout the country.

Nous remercions le Conseil des arts du Canada de son soutien. L'an dernier, le Conseil a investi 153 millions de dollars pour mettre de l'art dans la vie des Canadiennes et des Canadiens de tout le pays.

 Canada Council   Conseil des arts
for the Arts   du Canada

Printed and bound in Canada by Friesens
Design by Relish New Brand Experience
The author thanks William Dumas and Don Robertson for their assistance with the Cree language.

Library and Archives Canada Cataloguing in Publication

Robertson, David, 1977-, author
      When we were alone / David Alexander Robertson ; Julie Flett, illustrator.

ISBN 978-1-55379-673-2

    1. Native peoples—Canada—Residential schools—Comic books, strips, etc.
    2. Native peoples—Canada—Residential schools—Juvenile fiction.
    3. Graphic novels. I. Flett, Julie, illustrator II. Title.

PN6733.R63W44 2016   j741.5'971   C2016-904440-8

20 19 18 17   3 4 5 6 7

**HIGHWATER
PRESS**   www.highwaterpress.com
                 Winnipeg, Manitoba

Treaty 1 Territory and homeland of the Métis Nation.